Tidy Up Trevor

For Rhydian

A Red Fox Book

Published by Random House Children's Books,
20 Vauxhall Bridge Road, London SW1V 2SA.

First published in Great Britain by The Bodley Head 1993
Red Fox edition 1994

Copyright © Rob Lewis 1993

3 5 7 9 10 8 6 4

Printed in Hong kong

Rob Lewis has asserted his right to be identified as the author and
illustrator of this work in accordance with the Copyright, Designs and
Patents Act, 1988

RANDOM HOUSE UK Limited Reg. No. 954009

ISBN 0 09 920111 9

Tidy Up, Trevor

Rob Lewis

Red Fox

Trevor was bored.

On Monday he'd done a puzzle. On Tuesday he'd been roller skating. On Wednesday he'd painted pictures. On Thursday he'd played tennis. Now Trevor didn't know what to do. In the end, he did nothing.

'Do some digging and weeding,' said his dad.
  'Play with me,' begged his sister.
  'Read a book,' said his mum.
  'Just enjoy yourself, dear,' smiled his granny.

By lunchtime Trevor was still bored. He was bored and grumpy.

Dad was making sandwiches. 'Trevor will help,' said Mum.

'You're not doing anything, are you Trevor?'

'I know just the thing,' said Dad. 'A trip down the river will cheer you up.'

Trevor didn't want to go on a trip down the river.
By now, Mum was fed up too. 'If you're not coming
with us,' she said, 'you can go and tidy your cupboard.'

Trevor wished he had gone on the trip down the river.

He flumped down on the floor.

The cupboard door swung open, there were mountains of toys crammed inside. Trevor tugged at a box. Bump! Out fell a very bouncy ball, a bag of feathers, a game of Dingy Dungeons, three

jigsaws and a hard brown lump of Plasticine. It would take him a while to tidy up.

Trevor picked up the very bouncy ball. 'I wondered where that was,' he said to himself.

The trip down the river wasn't much fun. No one could forget about Trevor.
'I hope he's all right,' said Mum.

Trevor had found some knotty knitting and a crumpled kite.

The river curved under deep green leaves. 'I hope Trevor's being good,' said Dad.

Trevor had found his blue boat and a rubber ring.

It was time to go home. 'I wonder if Trevor has tidied his cupboard,' said his sister.

Trevor had found his train set and racing cars.

Back in the garden, Granny was snoring.
'Has Trevor been good?' asked Dad.
'Oh yes,' yawned Granny, 'as quiet as a mouse.'

'Trevor, we're home!' called Mum.
There was no answer.

'Trevor, what's all this mess?' Mum shouted.
There was still no answer.

The cupboard was tidy.

'Guess what, Mum,' said Trevor. 'I'm not bored any more.'

'Can I tidy up again tomorrow?'

Some bestselling Red Fox picture books

THE BIG ALFIE AND ANNIE ROSE STORYBOOK
by Shirley Hughes
OLD BEAR
by Jane Hissey
OI! GET OFF OUR TRAIN
by John Burningham
DON'T DO THAT!
by Tony Ross
NOT NOW, BERNARD
by David McKee
ALL JOIN IN
by Quentin Blake
THE WHALES' SONG
by Gary Blythe and Dyan Sheldon
JESUS' CHRISTMAS PARTY
by Nicholas Allan
THE PATCHWORK CAT
by Nicola Bayley and William Mayne
WILLY AND HUGH
by Anthony Browne
THE WINTER HEDGEHOG
by Ann and Reg Cartwright
A DARK, DARK TALE
by Ruth Brown
HARRY, THE DIRTY DOG
by Gene Zion and Margaret Bloy Graham
DR XARGLE'S BOOK OF EARTHLETS
by Jeanne Willis and Tony Ross
WHERE'S THE BABY?
by Pat Hutchins